Fr

Thirteen Short Stories

The glitch	3
Coming of age	8
The last journey	13
Franky	17
A scientist, kind of	24
Are you real?	30
I'm real	36
The philanthropist	39
The dream life	43
A hard working man	47
The end	51
The coder	56
The last match	63

The glitch

17th April

Today for the 3rd day in a row I woke up and the date is 15th April everywhere I look, from home to the timetable in the underground to everything in the office. My daily assignments are reappearing on my daily workflow board, even though I have no doubt I completed them the previous day. I have no idea what to attribute this phenomenon to. I´m keeping it to myself, who would take seriously something like that? The only person I think I can talk to about such an embarassing situation is my colleague Tony, he is into conspiracy theories, so I think he must have a plausible explanation and I can count on his confidentiality.

“Today is the 3rd day in a row, everything at home is working properly, I unplagged everything last nigh and plugged everything back in the morning to no result. Same thing here in the office, my pc, all the calendars, everything says 15th April.”

“I heard similar stories before, I believe that´s a further prove we are living in a simulation, what´s happening to you is either a glitch or you are going to be decomissioned quite soon.”
“Ok, I get the glitch, but what do you mean by ‘decommissioned’?”
“It means to be withdrawn from service, for you it means you´ll die. Depending on how the simulation evolves some characters become redundant, so they first become marginalized and later on they are deleted, you might get stuck on 15th April for months or even years before disappearing. Do you remember Robert, the tall guy? That’s probably why he disappeared leaving no trace.”
“That doesn’t sound good. And what about if it is a glitch?”
“If it is a glitch it will probably be fixed soon, normally within a week from the first time it happens. After work I´m contacting Morphy and see what can be done.”
“Who is Morphy?”
“He is the leader, for now you don´t need to know more.”

The meeting

Today I'm meeting Tony at a whitedwarf coffee shop and then we are meeting Morphy at an undisclosed location. I've never been before in this part of the city, the headquarter of the "Simhunters Organization" would be the ideal setting for a science fiction movie. A huge apparently dismissed warehouse containing a gigantic mainframe, servers and an army of screens and keyboards. Morphy is frantikally typing at one of the keyboards.

"So you've been stuck on the same date for a week?"

"Correct, I'm stuck on 15th April."

"I see, today is the 21st so, if you are just victim of a glitch from tomorrow everything should return to normality, otherwise we'll need to try an access to the upper level servers and check what your destiny will be. I need as much personal data from you as possible to start working on it, and if tomorrow you are still stucked on the 15th let me know as early as possible."

I'm really starting to worry now, nothing has changed from yesterday, I told Tony about it

and he informed Morphy in turn, we are going to meet him again at the headquarter.
"My friend, we found out what the problem is: it seems that your extremely low qualification and skills is not required anymore in this simulation, we must upgrade your position in the society otherwise you'll be certainly decommissioned. What would you like to be promoted to? A Huber driver, McPizza fast food?"
"Oh my God! Am I deemed so low a component of the society?"
"HaHaHa! Just kidding mate! I'm gonna change some parameters in the hierarchy of the company you supposedly work for and that will be it, tomorrow you will be alright."

I'm safe

Finally the situation has been unlocked, today everything has moved to 22nd April, I'm still not sure what all the story was about. Are we really in a simulation and Tony and Morphy saved me from being decommissioned? Was everything a sophisticated prank only? Perhaps we are all just hallucinating. The only thing I know for sure is that I owe many beers to Tony and Morphy.

Coming Of Age

Today I' m celebrating celebrating my 16th birthday, it is quite a milestone in the life of a Martian, because at twenty we come of age, so I need to start preparing everything from a legal point of view now if I want to be ready to get a vehicle conducting licence and be allowed to attend a university in four years time.

To start I must request the permission to travel to the central birth registry office on Earth to have a birth certificate, it could easily be requested from and mailed to Mars, but the interplanetary alliance government requires in person signature of the request on Earth to avoid fraud attempts from dodgy Martians. The first step to obtain the visa implies an interview of all my relatives currently living on Mars with the Earth Visas Enforcer. In my case they are only 12 people, my parents, my little sister, my uncle, my two aunts and all my cousins. The appointment with the enforcer was Sunday morning at 3 A.M. The appointments are always at night, and since the temperatures on Mars can go as low as

-100ºC, the probability that someone dies of hypothermia when venturing outside at night is extremely high. All this cumbersomeness is an effective way to discourage Martians from travelling to Earth. If all that wasn't enough trouble, my youngest cousin, Hanna, didn't remember my birthday when interrogated, the fact that she is only four years old didn't make the enforcer to consider for an exception. The appointment was rescheduled for the following day at 2 A.M. This time Hanna remembered the date and nobody died of hypothermia. The next step is the Martian Enforcer forwarding the request to the corresponding Earth Enforcer.

The response from Earth took six months to arrive, the permission was for a day in six months time, which makes a total of one year. Travelling to Earth with the new technologies is quite faster compared to when my grandmother moved to Mars, at the time the journey was around seven to eight months, nowadays it takes only a couple of months.

And here I´m on Earth! The planet is not the same as grandma used to tell me. Before she moved to Mars, Earth was a green planet where an infinity of animals lived peacefully, today is just a grey conglomerate of buildings and there is no trace of those gigantic herbivores grandma was so fond of.

Four months of my life wasted in a pointless trip to Earth. Now that I have my birthday certificate I can apply for a place at the university. The application comprises a fifty pages form, yes, fifty pages, with all my school history from first grade to date in a quite detailed way and a five thousand words statement explaining why I wish to join the university and what are my plans for the next twenty years, yes, twenty years, because according to the Interplanetary Alliance Government at seventeen years of age a person must know what will be doing at thirty -five.

In less than two years time I will be twenty years old, I must hurry up if I want to have the vehicle conducting licence soon after my birthday. The licence is an ancient tradition completely useless nowadays, vehicles are entirely automated and conducting one is down to choosing the destination on a screen once you are inside. Nevertheless at the conducting course people are taught several curious things, how to signal a direction change, for instance, or how to control the lubricating oil level in an internal combustion engine, even though nobody has ever seen such an engine on Mars. The point is that none of the components of the Mars local government has ever conducted a vehicle or has any technological knowledge, so they have literally no idea what all that stuff means, but the revenue from the tax on the licence issue is quite useful. To join the conducting school and the university I must provide four full body photos from four sides, my full genome sequence, all my fingers fingerprints and images of both my eyes irises. Some say that all that stuff is a little bit redundant, but once again, all that stuff is quite expensive and the economy rules.

First day at the university. The security staff are extremely meticulous on matching the DNA samples we must provide everyday to access the building, usually not less than an hour is needed, student's safety is paramount for the government. I don't know what the government is protecting me from, some years ago it was from "Foreign powers" but nobody on Mars really knew what that meant, so after a while the slogan became the more familiar “The enemy within.” Something went wrong with the sample I provided, it was retaken, in the end it took me two hours to get into the university building before starting any teaching activity. I’m starting now to understand the pessimistic attitude of some adult Martians, studying on Mars or doing something as simple as conducting a vehicle has become a struggle against bureaucracy and expenses, no wonder young Martians are devoting themselves to interplanetary trafficking and other illegal activities instead of pursuing an academic or professional career.

The Last Journey

Year 2300, the last humans on Hearth are embarking for the last journey of the Mars L Cruiser. Olivia never travelled outside Earth in her life, she always thought that Earth was beautiful and wanted to live there, even after humans managed to destroy almost every form of life through nuclear war and overexploitation of natural resources. The study of the few remaining natural beauties, millennia old human artifacts and monuments that hinted at how great life on Earth was before the WWIII, kept Olivia on a constant state of awe and admiration for her native planet. Olivia often dreams of green fields and rivers, but will never know what was it like the live view of those majestic trees and animals once populated Earth: elephants, giraffes, horses, cows, pigs. She often fantasizes about the planet going back to the old splendour of the 21st century she knows only from books and movies, thanks to the commitment of the powerful of the solar system, but those remain a young girl dreams only, nobody really cares about life on Earth.

Somehow terraforming Mars and the Moon turned out to be cheaper than trying to reclaim the mostly uninhabitable planet Earth, or maybe it was just more convenient to the "Interplanetary Contractors LTD." The Mars L Cruiser space ship is departing for the last time from Earth with the last 2000 humans on board, there is no way back, the interplanetary airport is being decommissioned. The journey will be seven months long, a real nightmare, made even worst by the complete absence of any window or opening to the exterior on the ship, making it the modern equivalent of a cattle wagon.

Most of the people on board are enthusiastic about their journey, none of them visited Mars before and communication between the two planets is heavily censored for security reasons. The most often mentioned advantage of life on Mars is "living life with dignity", humans didn't care about living a dignified life on Earth, actually didn´t care about life on Earth at all but, apparently, dignity became the main principle of life on Mars. Olivia is quite suspicious about this sudden love of humans for dignity.

“You’ll start going to school again, you will make new friends, aren’t you happy?” Repeats everyday Olivia’s mum trying to cheer her up.
“Are there animals on Mars?” Is Olivia’s usual reply.
"I don’t know, we’ll find out soon.” Terminates the conversation.

It turns out that life on Mars is not as dignified as terrestrials where made to believe, conferming Olivia’s suspicion. Terraforming the planet is a process still in the making, the lower gravity on Mars makes walking difficult and causes osteoporosis from a young age on martians, breathing is something completely different from what it was on Earth, the air tastes and smells weird. There are also issues and health problems due to the different forms of cosmic radiation and… there are no animals on Mars. The only thing Olivia finds interesting on Mars is food, even though it tastes terrible, is real food and not laboratory grown flavourless white powder mixed with poisoned water.

Years go by and Olivia´s dreams about Earth are becoming less frequent, time is doing its job, Martians believe the stories about the blue marble full of life are legends, propaganda and the records department are doing an excellent job. The promise of the paradise on Mars never materialized, Olivia made a family and got children and grandchildren and they loved to hear the stories about Earth from grandma. When talks about explorative missions to check the health of Earth, in case a back up planet would become necessary, Olivia was not among us anymore. Her grandchildren promised to take her back to Earth one day.

Franky

Trip to Earth

After the Third World War a great number of humans died and the survivors moved to the Moon. More than a century later, from 1st January 2222, Lunatics are allowed to visit Earth for research purposes. Leonardo and Sofia obtained permission for a trip from the Open Moon University Historical Archaeology Department. Their project consists in gathering as much data as possible from the archaic hard drives ubiquitous on the planet. The data might be used to create sims and try to learn from them about the mistakes that destroyed almost all forms of life on Earth and made it uninhabitable.

After all this time Earth is still uninhabitable, the radiation levels are down to the pre war levels, but fauna and flora were almost completely wiped out, fungi were the best equipped to resist radiation and are now the dominant species on the planet. The spectacle is terrifying: megacities, skyscrapers, bridges but no life. After finding the right connector cable model for some laptops found in an electronics retail and repair shop, Leonardo and Sofia started crawling the data.

“Terrestrials seemed to be extremely self-conscious beings.” Observed Lorenzo.

“Yep, obsessed with their organic shell and those horrible and noisy petrol powered vehicles.” Added Sofia.

“And guns. Look at this guy! Franky, he described himself as a bodybuilder.”

“Wow! He looked quite good, actually. We could use his pictures and videos to create a sim. He also kept personal and professional journals, a Facebook page, a Tinder profile and thousands of pictures in different devices. This is the right subject for the respawn project.”

Back home

Back home the two students uploaded all the data regarding Franky to the Great Cloud and created the Sim Franky, probably the first ever constructed using data from a real Terrestrial. Leonardo and Sofia hope to gain some insight about what the last moments of Earth were like. Many questions needed answers about the sims created with the latest technology, are sims conscious? If they are, are sims and the original organic beings the data was gathered from the same person? Are they two completely different entities? What could be the legal status of a conscious sim? And many more.

Sim Franky is ready to be interrogated.

"What's your name?"

"Franklin Jones Smith, people call me Franky."

"I'm Sofia, nice to meet you, Franky. How old are?"

"I'm thirty-five years old."

"And where are you from?"

"I always lived in England but… this place feels quite odd."

"It is because we are on the Moon now, Earth was destroyed over a century ago by a World nuclear conflict. Do you have any memories about it?"

"I'm obviously dreaming… yes, I remember the news about the first nuclear strike, but it was just few days ago, not a century."

Sim Franky was behaving as expected, he had no knowledge about what happened after the nuclear strikes, his life was abruptly interrupted than and electronically restarted today.
“So how come I’m alive after all this time?”
This was a crucial moment, Sofia had to tell Sim Franky that he was a digital copy of the human Franky, that his brain was a very accurate copy of the original, made of artificial neural networks instead of organic material. Some would say he was a silicon based form of life.
“To keep it short, you are an AI reconstruction of the original you who lived on Earth, we uploaded all the data we could find about you to the Great Cloud to make a Sim, that is you.”
“I still think I’m dreaming, anyway, if what you say is true, it means all the science fiction stories about brain implants, brain transplants and simulated reality and so on, kind of become real.”
“Somehow that’s correct. Would you like to answer some questions about your time on Earth?”

"Sure! It seems that my life from now on won't be much interesting, so why not to indulge in nostalgia and recall the good times."
The ease with which Sim Franky accepted the fact that he was a digital entity, casts some doubt about Sim Franky's consciousness. It should be shocking and terrifying to learn about your own death and... rebirth, but he didn't seem to care much.
"Do you remember what was the reason for the nuclear conflict?"
"Well, I'm just a normal guy, you know. People like me didn't have much of a say in such big international issues… the last thing I remember that might be related to your question, was some long term tensions in the centre regions of the Eurasian Nation, there had been decades of nuclear threat talks, it seems that at the end they found a reason to nuke each other."
"What can you tell us about the climate change issues, it seems people completely ignored it, even though it was the second most likely cause for the destruction of life on the planet."
"Again, not much to say from my point of view, but, all along the 21st century taxation on

renewable energy power plants steadily grew, conversely the taxation on fossil fuels decreased, at some point it wasn't financially feasible the use of the renewables. Can I make some questions now?"
"Sure you can."
"Do you know what happened to Alexandra?"
"I'm sorry but we don't know anything about her. Who is Alexandra?"
"She is my girlfriend. 'She that was ever fair and never proud, had tongue at will and yet was never loud.' As the Bard said. We are making big plans for the future, saving money for a home, thinking about having kids. Once again, if what you are saying about the destruction of Earth is correct, she must be gone also. Might you be able to do with her the same trick you did with me? I mean to recreate her in here?"
Here something interesting was happening, Sim Franky is showing some emotion or feeling, or something a Lunatic science student could think was such.
"If you cannot do that, there is no point in me being here, you should switch off this thing after you asked everything you need to know from me."

Even though Sim Franky didn't have a legal person status, Leonardo and Sofia considered him to be conscious, and decided to respect his will of being switched off. The 1st of February 2222, Sim Franky, the first TerraSim ever created, was 'switched off'.

A Scientist, Kind of

On the Moon

It was a Sunday morning when Noha Muller found himself sleeping on a bench in Sun Square in Small City on the Moon. That was a big problem, he wasn't carrying any personal document with him and didn't know hot to get back to the Earth, but more than anything, he didn't have an idea on how and why he went there. The only thing Noha knew for sure was that he had to reach the interplanetary airport and then make something up. Lunatics are not famous for being welcoming towards Terrestrials, and not having how to prove his identity and status on the planet didn't help.

Elias was probably right when he warned me about the dangers of the quantum superposition simulations. I can' t think of any plausible explanation to my situation other than something going wrong with the isolation of the quantum computer observation machinery, yea, cheap second hand stuff, and these are the consequences."

"Good morning Sir, one way to Earth, please."

"Can I see your ID card, Sir?"
"I'm afraid I left it home…"
"Oh really? That's too bad! You must go back home and take it."
"Well, my home is on Earth, actually."
"Oh I see, so you came to the Moon without any kind of identification document or visa? You will explain why to the police."

Monday

"Sure, you are scientist from Earth… did you drink alcohol last night? What about mushrooms? I heard they are pretty good down there."

"I'm not drunk and I'm not on drugs!" Noha complained, to great amusement of the presents.

"Illegal immigration is a serious crime here on the Moon, tomorrow you will know your fate." Concluded Mr. Justice.

And the judgment was indeed unexpectedly harsh. "Before sending you back to Earth, we will dye your hair the colours of the glorious flag of the sovereign state of the Moon and you will have to wear a Nickelback T-shirt for the journey; since this is the first time you are coming as an illegal to the Moon, mitigating circumstances are accepted so you will not have to wear a red cap," sentenced Mr. Justice.

Back Home

"I told you to be careful with that stuff, one of this days you will end up killing yourself!" Said Elias while shaving Noha's head.

"I didn't imagine something like that could happen so easily, you know the probabilities of that happening have many zeros after the coma, right?"

"Yes I know, maybe at the upper level are cutting the financing for the maintenance and the simulation we are in, so is not working properly anymore, you might be on the brink of something with your simulations, but that something may cost you your life."

The following day two diplomats dressed completely in black and with necks larger than the head, visited Noha at his apartment.

"We have no track of your journey to the Moon but you were reearthed from there as

an illegal, you must tell us what´s going on here."
"I´m not sure about what´s going on but, I think the machines over there might be somehow responsible for my trip to the Moon."
"Really? What are those machines?"
"They are parts of a quantum computer, the only way I can explain my appearance on the Moon is that a simulation about quantum superposition I was running on them escaped the machines and expanded into the room while I was sleeping, taking me to the Moon."
"We have no idea what all that means, you will explain it to the migration office director."

At the director's office

"What you are describing sounds like you were teleported from your moulded disgusting bedroom to the Moon."
"Yes Sir, you can say that."
"Would you be able to reproduce the experiment you were doing when that happened?"

"I might be able to do it, but it could be unpredictable and dangerous."
"The choice is yours, you can repeat the experiment under my supervision or be tried for high treason and spend the rest of your life, five or six months, mining cobalt and titanium on Mars."
"I´m grateful to be given the opportunity to choose, even though I find the Martian option quite alluring, I think I'll try to reproduce the experiment under your supervision."
"I think that's the right thing to do, the two gentlemen you already know will keep you company tonight, I'll see you tomorrow morning at your hovel."

Repeating the experiment

Everything is ready to restart the simulation, when the officer arrives I'll only have to press start and… boom! Now let's wear the suite.
"Everything is ready, I can restart the simulation and see what happens."
"Are you sure is not dangerous?"
"I swear on my mother's life you have nothing to fear."

"If so, why are you wearing that weird space suite?"
"I'm wearing it because I'm touching the processor of the quantum computer, you have nothing to fear."
"Right, you can restart it now but be careful with what you do, keep in mind the Mars holiday option."

Of course I was lying when I said there was no danger, after two minutes from starting the "simulation" all forms of life disappeared from the room, except the only one wearing the lead-titanium suite, exactly as predicted by the calculations made with Elias. Will the gentlemen be reearthed from the Moon or from Mars as illegals in the following days? If the math is right, they will not.

Are You Real?

State of affairs

That girl really looks unreal, I'm quite sure she is not an organic being but just a droid. Look at how she pretends to know the difference between the different varieties of apples and pears. She is very good looking, too beautiful to be real. She has been carefully programmed to act as a real woman, now she is even scratching her head in front of the apples to give the impression that she is in doubt about which ones to buy, I guess she realized I'm looking at her and she's upping up the ante. I know she will just buy the food and throw it away or give it to the homeless in her neighbourhood. She is not the only dummy inside the hypermarket today. Look at the man restocking the liquors shelf, the colour of his skin is absolutely unnatural. I'm not coming back to this shop anymore, they are everywhere! Even fake disable people on wheelchairs now!

I wish I could travel back in time, to the good old times of the 21st century, before humans started moving to other planets, before AGI developments allowed mock humans to become autonomous and almost undistinguishable from real humans. The government is beyond a shadow of doubt responsible for the situation, it made a big mistake granting false humans citizenship status fifty years ago. But I know the real reason behind all this, the government wants to replace all humans on Earth with cyborgs, they are resistant to cosmic radiation and that makes them usable on Earth and relocatable to Mars, they can work longer shifts than humans and more important than anything, they are programmable and if something goes wrong, they can just be switched off.

Not even at home I can be sure a simulacrum is not checking on me. My neighbour Franky, for instance, he says he is a bodybuilder and that's why he is so muscular, but I think he is just a prototype of a new robot model. I'm quite sure even my daughter Marie is a double, she is very good at school and she is passionate about science, and that's a detail that gives her away, we all know that science is just part of the conspiracy! Probably the real Marie was exchanged at birth in the hospital without my wife and me noticing anything. I still need to figure out many things about Marie, how is it possible to make her eat, digest and have all the other human bodily functions, how they manage to make her grow? there must be a great deal of secret technologies that allow all that.

Going to work by subway doesn't exempt me from the prosecution. Those two things at the other end of the carriage are ostentatiously looking the other way, but from the way they are laughing it is clear that they are talking about me, 'The human'.

At the workplace things aren't any better. The guy usually sitting next to me is clearly a counterfeit, I don't believe a human can type so fast and make no errors, he is almost always the best performer in the office. A couple of days ago he pretended to cut himself with scissors and he was bleeding, it seems that the secret technology not only allows them to fake all human bodily functions but also to 'bleed'. One more thing that I find absolutely unbelievable about him is his perennial smiling face, that's clearly a non human trait, why should people be smiling all day long while working?

Last week my wife insisted on me going to the doctor to see what can be done about my anxiety, he prescribed me a substance called fluoxetine, but since I know that almost everything around me is part of the plot I'm just pretending to swallow the pills, they will not get me that easily.

Even going to the restaurant has become a nightmare, the waiters look like they are not locals, but that's just a trick to mask the reality, they are doppelgängers. No surprise they are extremely friendly with Marie.

Let's talk animals. Have you seen the Pisterliner dogs? Nobody will convince me that they are real dogs, same goes for the Chat de Bordeaux cats.

The Moment of Truth

And the day I'm proving I'm not crazy is here. The day I'm unmasking the great global conspiracy has arrived. I'm going to the toilet, nobody suspects anything, there it is the fire sprinkler, exactly above the cubicle I'm in, let's stand on the wc and warm up the fire sprinkler, this will make the fire alarm go off and those electronic machines pretending to be humans will be fucked.

Clearly the technology owned by the conspirators is top of the notch, the droids can grow as humans do, they can bleed and they are also water proof. The motherfuckers just behaved exactly as humans would do in such circumstances, some were panicking because of the fire alarm, some were just laughing and making silly jokes about how much water they were going to save having a free shower at the workplace, the only thing that didn't happen was what I expected, the monsters caching fire because of the electrical short circuits induced by the water.

The End of History

It seems that we reached the point of no return with the substitution, even though I haven't been able to prove it, most of the 'people' around me are not real. Most of the patriots of the old good times gave up the fight, nobody is trying anymore to defend the natural rights of the real human beings, some old friends are even dismissing my complaints as madness. I guess the best thing to do would be to disappear without leaving a trace and move to the Moon or Mars and start a new life. Up there only humans are allowed, they did not make the mistake of granting non humans human rights and access to the planet… yet.

I'm Real

The human over there is looking at me in a strange way, maybe he finds me attractive, or maybe he suspects I'm a sim, let's pretend I'm choosing the apples, yes, scratching my head like this should do, apples or pears? While walking out of the shop I say a quick hello to the sim stocking up the shelves, he must be a first generation model. The situation on the planet is getting out of hand, humans are becoming more intolerant towards sims by the day. The creation of sims and AGI is a human idea and they greatly benefitted from it, but somehow they lost control of it and now they are complaining about sims rights and AGI taking their jobs. Shouldn't they have thought about it when everything was at the beginning, maybe when it was enough to switch off a server or two to avoid problems and sims inhabited only video games played on boolean machines? Of course humans think it has to be government fault, as always. You are beyond the Pillars of Hercules, dear humans, and now you don't know how to come back.

I'm gonna give this food to the humans living opposite my appartment, they are unemployed and have a kid, other humans are not that keen on helping them, it seems. They graciously thanked me, "You are a really good *human.*" They said, smiling like they meant it.

"Indeed, I'm *real.*" I replied.

A really common misconception among humans is that sims are planning some kind of revolutionary power grab which, by the way, we could easily and succesfully carry out. Why should we want to become Presidents, Prime Ministers, Popes or anything like that? Humans don´t understand a basic difference between us and them, we are not built to be egocentric, proud or vain, we are just made to do things and programmed to avoid damaging other sims and humans. I often hear humans talking about moving to other planets, horrible places like Mars because over there sims are not allowed, or travelling back in time if it was possible. Basically for many humans the main point in life is not how good life is but how far away the "others" are. Extreme acts of intolerance are being carried out. Some days ago a human tried to kill his coworkers and stated that “everybody in there is part of the conspiracy!” When arrested.

The philanthropist

Together we can make it!

The presentation of the new Jonathan Dawson's Charity initiatives has been hugely successful. Particularly, the project for the new homeless shelter caused a stir, never before a non governmental institution diverted so much resources(money) into a philanthropic initiative in this town. The initiative is not only directed at helping homeless people to improve their lives, but also at creating occupational and professional opportunities through extensive training provided to the people willing to make a difference in our society, as punctually stated the charity trustee Mr. Jonathan Dawson Jr. "Together we can make it!"

"Wow! That was really something! I can take off the VR headset for today. Let's have a look at the JODATech last quarter performance. Not good, total revenue up only 10% and profits before tax at a miserable 20 billion Earth Dollars. At this pace it will take me several months to buy a gilded castle for my wife's chihuahua, a promise is a promise. Some cuts need to be done to the staff budget for the Moon market, bloody expensive bastards up there! They have to understand that the cuts must be done to counteract the economic decline on the planet and that by doing it, the universe will become a better place… for myself. We might also blame the immigrants from earth or any other minority about the worsening economy, everybody hates minorities! It always works."

The featured article on the front page on the "Financial Moon" today: "The Moon government steps in to tackle the decline in investments on the planet from Earth investors." One trillion Moon Dollars will be spent in the next two years to create and renovate physical assets; amongst others, a new interplanetary airport, a new uranium and thorium mining facility. "The mining of the rare earths is a necessary evil, it is something that needs to be done if we want to make our planet a better place. Together we can make it!" Punctually stated the Moon governor Mr. Joseph Dawson.

One year later

The demonstrations on the Moon are challenging the democratic institutions of the Double Planet Alliance. The working conditions in the new mines are inhuman, salaries are even lower than the equivalent job on Earth, and it seems that Lunatics are a fierce and brave population not willing to cooperate. The negotiation is at a stalemate.

"Why can't they just modify the algorithm that controls them to make them accept the working conditions?" Insisted Mr. Jonathan Dawson Jr.

"Because they are not sims, Sir. They are organic beings living in a physical world, as you and me."

"Do you mean they are humans?"

"Yes Sir, that's what I mean."

"I hate humans! Life is much easier wearing VR headsets. What they are forgetting up there is that the artificial atmosphere on the Moon is owned and operated by the JODATech, tomorrow this time I'm quite sure it will malfunction. Can you organize the substitutes together with the operations

manager at the of JODATech Droids division?"
"I will Take care of everything, Sir."
"Thank you Jeeves. Now let me go back to my VR thing."
The main article on the "Financial Moon" today: "JODATech apologizes for the Issues to the Moon atmosphere that killed over one million Lunatics, the company will work hard in collaboration with the Moon government to avoid such tragedies in the future. Our heartfelt prayers go out to the victims and their families."

The dream life

A life well lived

Gabriel lives a happy life in the small town in the Alps-Maritime department where he was born 35 years ago. He happily goes to work everyday in the local small branch of one of the biggest banks in Europe, not possible to get a better job around there. Financial crisis are something that doesn't bother him, they usually are a good boost to the finances of people who know how to deal with them, actually. Gabriel can't complain about his private life either, happily married to his sweetheart of the college days, Louise. They have a beautifull six years old daughter, Ambre, who attends the first year in the local primary school and whos performance is up to par with her parents expectations and reputation. They live in a beautifully renovated mas with a huge swimming pool and vineyard. They conduct what most people in the world would say it's a dream life, playing tennis after work on Thursdays, restaurant on Fridays, cinema on Saturdays, trip to the seaside on

Sundays and so on. He could purchase a more expensive sport car, but he is a humble guy, he wouldn't feel at ease driving it in a small town where everybody knows everybody. The family business, wine production, is another motive for satisfaction in Gabriel's life. Sometimes he wonders about leaving his employment at the bank to help his elderly parents run the company, but he is not sure he is generous enough to deal with the workers in the vineyard and winery.

The awakening

Monsieur Raphaël woke up startled and sweating like never before in his life. He had a nightmare in which he was a rich man who made big money through financial speculation, taking advantage of people in financial distress and exploiting workers in the family vineyard and winery. Madame Alba reassured him and found the dream quite amusing.

"Do not worry, I'm sure you will never be anything like that." Madame Alba insisted.

Monsieur Raphaël tried to go on about his day as he usual did, but something on the back of his mind wasn't completely right, maybe the dream really meant something or was a signal from who knows who or what. Philosophical and ethical questions tormented Monsieur Raphaël all the morning, was the rich guy attitude towards his employees and clients correct? Was the Monsieur Raphaël we all know dreaming of being the rich guy, or was he the rich guy dreaming of being Monsieur Raphaël? But the most unsettling question tormenting him was: "Is there a way to know for sure who I am, or will I spend the rest of my life in doubt?"

At the end of the morning, Monsieur Raphaël decided that all this questioning reality and societal rules wasn't suitable for someone in his position. After feeding himself from an excellent cow's carrion he could choose between blueberries and redberries, but he couldn't see a reason for having one instead of the other, they are equally tasty and nutritious so he had both. After lunch he really needed some wallowing in mud, and after the skin care he dedicated the afternoon to collecting branches to make the nest a bit more comfy and more suitable to his main activity in life, which was procreating. In conclusion of the day, the last thing that went through Monsieur Raphaël mind before getting asleep, was a dictum from an illustrious compatriot of him whose name he couldn’t remember: *Coito, ergo sum.*

A Hard Working Man

A day in the office

A hard day at the office today, I made over four thousand mouse clicks and almost all of them were made in the correct box. I logged into several different online platforms using the seven factor authentication nearly twenty times and, last but not least, I've been identified by security staff over ten times for no reason. This is what we call "a productive day" at JODATech.

I consider myself to be a lucky person, I really love my job. It consists of carefully following instruction on what to click on a screen, for instance a voice might tell me on the headset something like 'click the circle' while on my screen appear a circle and a square, in this case my job would be to click the circle, but in case of doubt I can always consult an extensive and detailed knowledge base archive. While at first it may not sound appealing, I love it because my operations are of the utmost important for the company AGI systems security.

Another day in the office

Bad news from the office today. A meeting is scheduled at 9 a.m. into the deputy substitute of the deputy director office, and when such a high rank of the company hierarchy is involved, nothing good is coming, the last time I heard about such a meeting, ten thousand people lost their jobs on Earth.

"We need to understand how such a serious mistake can be made. Was your headset working properly? Did you hear the voice say 'click the crimson circle'?"

"Yes Sir, I clearly heard the voice say 'click the crimson circle'."

"If so, why did you click the red circle?"

"I guess because red and crimson are very similar colours."

"Probably you don't understand how serious your situation is. Do you really think that crimson and red are very similar colours?"

"Yes Sir, I really think that red and crimson are very similar colours."

"You will have to bear the consequences of your answer for the rest of your life, so I'm asking for the last time, do you really think

that red and crimson are very similar colours?"
"Yes Sir, I really think that red and crimson are very similar colours and probably that led to me erroneously clicking the red circle instead of the crimson circle."
"I'm really disappointed by your behaviour, I was told you were extremely familiar with the procedures that regulate you duties, but that is clearly not the case. Since you are convinced that red and crimson are very similar colours, you are relieved from your duties from this very moment, you will know your new position in the company next week."

And that was the end of my exciting career, from age twenty-two I was doomed to do menial pointless basic controls to the end of my working life.

Fifty years later

"The last working day in my life hasn't been as sad as I expected. For the last two years, after Elias moved to the Moon, I've been the only organic being working at JODATech Droids Division, so the social interactions everybody enjoyed decades ago didn't exists any more. The AGI systems do not need any more human coaching, so my role in the office was just controlling the stock of thorium for the nuclear reactor that provides the energy for the Droids production, task that can now easily be done by the cheapest entry level droid. Life on Earth has become quite boring, machines manage their own stuff in mysterious ways, surveillance on humans is carried out 24 hours a day, it is not possible to leave home without being followed by a camera drone. The few surviving humans moved to the Moon and the even fewer still here are elderly too sick or too tired of life to try a new start. Elias insists on me moving there, at least it is possible enjoy a semblance of real life and probably that's what I'm going to do."

The End

December 12 2112.

I'm driving home after the usual wonderful day at the office, usual anonymous song playing on the songs generator interrupted by the announcement: "the Eurasian Nation launched a massive nuclear strike against the Terrorists Countries, the Terrorists Countries are expected to counterattack within minutes." And I knew from the first moment what all that meant.

The proliferation of nuclear weapons turned out to be more MAD than everybody predicted for the last century and half. The second strike from the Terrorists Countries was efficiently completed to great satisfaction of the President and his entourage. Satisfaction short lived since the whole continent and all its population were wiped out in less then one hour. The Iberian Peninsula is somehow far away from the decision-making centres in the Eurasian Nation and that is giving us some extra days or maybe weeks to live, maybe I will see year 2113.

January 12 2113

I made it to the new year. The levels of radiation are probably peaking now, causing an increase in miscarriages and thyroid dysfunctions among other diseases we are no more able to treat. The temperatures dropped significantly after the conflict because of the nuclear fallout, for the same reason the production of energy using photovoltaic panels the Peninsula relied on, is heavily compromised. Ironically, civilian nuclear power was deemed unsafe along the 21st century and most of the reactors dismantled... now we know what the uranium was actually needed for. This will not only be the last, longest winter of humanity but also the coldest one.

Not much is known at the moment about the consequences of the second strikes on the Eastern regions, the net is heavily damaged and the civilian satellites orbiting in LEO stopped working. Probably, there aren't many survivors to operate or repair the net around there. Rumours are spreading about westward mass movement of people from the central regions, but the truth is that most of them are dying from the radiation effects, probably the much feared invasion of refugees won't happen.

The end is here, food is almost finished, almost nothing is growing in the greenhouses, the temperatures are too low to allow anything to grow, water is poisoned, rain is radioactive, the sunlight is almost completely absent. I have increasing difficulty breathing and I lost almost completely my hair. All in all I'm one of the "lucky" ones, I'm not witnessing my mother, my wife or my children rotting alive or starving to death. Some are leaving and trying their fortune travelling eastwards, nobody really believes it's a good idea, it's just a way to keep some hope alive, probably is better than waiting for death here. This might be the last page of the diary.

Fuck Mondays

I'm normally exited about checking the evolution of the multiple simulations I'm running on the college servers, but going to college on Mondays is always a nightmare and today is no exception. That pool party yesterday was so much fun but probably I shouldn't have drank that much.

In some of the simulated worlds the sims developed extremely advanced technologies in a short time. In roughly 8 million Earth years they went from splitting off the evolution line from other primates to an interplanetary species. In one subset of simulations the algorithm is tweaked so as to allow the self destruction, we normally stop the simulation before that happens to save time and not having to start a new set, but today I'm too tired to care about it. Of course the sims didn't waste such an opportunity to destroy everything! I'm fucking tired of having to restart all this shit on a monthly basis! But that's what the boss wants and if I want to get that bloody college degree I must keep pleasing him. Next time I will reduce the self destruction probability parameter by let's say 50%, or maybe 60% and hope that the old man doesn't check that value.

Upper Floor

The situation with the simulations run by students is getting out of hand. The computational power at their disposal is so high that anyone can run thousands of simulation and the sims in the simulation can in turn run their own simulation with quite bizarre results. One of the sims run a simulation in which the simulated biological evolution created an interplanetary species able to construct mass destruction weapons! What a nonsense and waste of resources! Maybe the financing should be redirected to more sensible activities.

The coder

Day by day

At JODATech Gaming we are working on the new version of "Insignificant City", the 25th iteration, to be precise. The game is based on normal everyday activities like walking, using public transport, shopping for groceries. The player accumulates points from this activities and if she reaches the daily threshold can move to the next level where there are more daily activities to choose from. When the game was presented 25 years ago, it wasn't a great success, most of the reviewers deemed it doomed from the start, but they didn't know how much the new technologies would change society in the following couple of decades. In year 2030, when the first version of the game was introduced, it was still normal to go to work in the company premises, or leave home to buy food etc. But thanks to manufacturing automation and the development of what is commonly known as "web 5.0", nowadays there isn't much of a need for people to move around to be productive, or maybe there isn't a need for people at all. That's why the game popularity has increased so much with time, younger generations find it weird and amusing experiencing simulated interactions in VR with shopkeepers, taxi drivers or any other human they do not have a kinship bond with.

I still enjoy occasionally working from the office, it forces me to do some walking, talking to the old school colleagues who still go to the office as I do and taking the few buses still operating in the city. I normally take the bus D75, the number gives an idea of how many lines where in operation in the past, today only two survive in my city, the other one is the N79. The local government keeps some humans driving them but that wouldn't be necessary, they could easily buy new completely autonomous machines as in many other cities. The driver today looks somehow familiar, maybe I've seen him the last time I came to the office. I'm the only person onboard, strangely this bus doesn't have any sits, it is completely empty internally, I' ll get home in a few minutes so that's not a problem, but still is something really weird. I currently live in the Mega Ivory Tower number two, at the 178th floor from where I have an amazing view of the Mega Ivory Tower number one. The usual two boxes of groceries I ordered are outside my apartment door as always, I unlock the door and when lifting the boxes they feel extremely light, one of them turns out to be empty, I don't remember such a thing happening before. After dinner I relax playing Soccer55 online, real ball team sports are something that almost completely disappeared. Once again, people don't enjoy meeting others in large groups and prefer to do individual physical activities like running on treadmills or stationary bicycles. Nevertheless people playing Soccer55 online call themselves "football players" despite the fact that they never kicked a real ball in their lives.

At work we are working on increasing the availability and variety of public transport as the levels of "Insignificant City" grow. We are working really hard on adding buses, underground lines, some very realistic taxis etc. We are also working on merging it with Soccer55 and make it available at the highest level, that would make it even easier for players spend most of their spare time hooked into JODATech Gaming VR universe, without even the need to login into two different games.

Today is my self-imposed weekly working day from the company premises, as always I enjoy having a chat with real people, or having a junk food snack and a watery coffee from the vending machines in the office. Every time I work from the office less people is there, will be no surprise if in a few months I will be the only one doing it, what will I do at that point? Time will say. I catch the usual D75 in the evening to go home, I'm not really sure but it seems the driver is the same man that was driving last week and today the bus is not empty as it was last time, normal seats and a couple of passengers are on it... well the seats look exactly the same as the ones we drew for the game, the upholstey pattern is exactly the same, I made it, clearly someone is saving money on design and copied them from us. Usual two boxes of groceries by the door and once again one of them is empty, I will complain with the delivery company this time. And to avoid any change to my daily routine, let's have a look at the latest update of Soccer55 before going to sleep.

One more thing in the game is being copied from real life: groceries delivered at home. I'm kind of puzzled by this evolution of the game, I always thought that the interesting part of it was to do in VR things that people are not used to do anymore in real life, not sure what the point in replicating boring everyday activities we all do is. Whatever… let's provide the riders with fancy coloured bycicles and let's draw some food to fill up the boxes, straight bananas, non-alcoholic beer and decaffeinated coffee… sometimes I'm hilarious!

Weekly trip to the office. The few people over there today complained about the lack of support from the company to people willing to work in presence instead of remotely, and about real public transport getting progressively less efficient. It is possible that the next time I go there I will be the only one in the building. Usual bus and usual driver in the evening. I don't know why but there is a third box of groceries outside the door at home, I unlock the door and get inside, I'm curious about the third box, I open it, it contains non-alcoholic beer and decaffeinated coffee, this can only be a present from a colleague trying to be funny.

Something is not right

For some months now I'm having a very difficult to explain and uncomfortable feeling, maybe I'm working to much on VR and video games and I need a holiday. More or less the point is the following: my private life is getting progressively more similar to the life in the VR environment I'm building at work, and I don't mean the surface of my lifestyle or the general look of the city I live in, which we reproduced on the VR platforms, I mean specific events, like last night in the pub with a couple of friends where the band looked exactly as the one we inserted into some levels of "Insignificant City" and played exactly the same tunes; an other example is the bus I use to commute on, exact copy of the ones we drew for the games, and even more little details like the food in the supermarkets, the bicycles used by delivery riders and many others, they are all exact copies of virtual stuff. All this really worries me, what will be the point of life when everything will be done in virtual reality, when everybody will be able to become whatever they want just spending few virtuacoins on a gaming VR platform? Music star? Olympic champion? Nobel prize? Just put your credit card number and buy it.

I've been talking about my existential crisis with Niklas, an old friend, and he expressed the same feelings about VR and real life merging into one, he didn't want to mention it explicitly, but he thinks we went beyond that already. My guess is that he thinks we are living in a simul-…

The simulation HAL2055 has been deactivated. The purpose of the project, verifying the ability of sims to find out they were living in a simulation, has been achieved.

The last match

Today's match decides if we are going to be relegated to second regional division in the Rugby Regional Championship. We' ve been promoted last year to the first division against the odds, nobody expected "The Fat Sloths" to win the second division, even less to survive more than one season in the top division. But once again we are fighting for it and believe me, there is nothing in this world you should fear more than a forty years old fat guy, playing what he knows is the last Rugby match in his life.

And what a match it was! We made it! We are not being relegated! I don't remember running so much in the hundreds of matches played in my whole life, or making so much tackles in one match. Mathew, another fat old guy playing his last match, got the ball a couple of metres from the goal line, turned slightly his head to the right and I was there, he passed me the ball and I just had to dive and score the last try of my life.

That match made me kind of a celebrity, the following year I became the head coach of the team, local radios and magazines interviewed me, life was good, my family grew, years went by without me noticing. Rugby is no more the sport I played and loved, professionalism changed it a lot, there are no more fat guys playing just for fun like in the old days, nowadays most of the players are very skilled man-mountain athletes. Memories fade year after year, but not the ones about that day, that match and Mathew passing that ball.

I have three grandchildren, luckily none of them is interested in Rugby, I wouldn't be happy seeing them play such a violent sport it has become today. Two of them are university students, it seems they are really good ones. Occasionally they tell me something about the modern science and technology they are working on, stuff that was science fiction when I was their age is now available and they are trying to understand how to make a good use of it. The last time we met they told me about some weird stuff I didn't want to believe, I thought they were trying to make me a fool, but in the following days the news started talking about it, that made me change my mind, almost. Now I' m trying to write the concept as I understood it: it seems that today is possible to mess up with the human's brain in a way that people can relive some past experiences or even have memories altered, follows that if in the same community enough memories are tampered, it is to some extent the equivalent of rewriting the history of the community itself. I don't really like the idea of a group of scientists being able to "rewrite history", but the idea of being one more time the Rugby player, before leaving for ever, it is not something I can or I want to resist, and I'm gonna drag Mathew down into it with me.

I persuaded Mathew to volunteer for the experiments. I specifically requested if it was possible to relive "that match" with Mathew, they say it is possible, the only problem is the synchronization of thought between the two, I know that won't be a problem for us. The preparation was long and scary, we are wearing helmets connected to what looks like a big mainframe or server or something like that, when all the gear was in place we were made to drink a disgusting stuff that would improve chemical activity of the synapses, that's what I understood, anyway. There we are running around on the field, chasing the ball, making tackles, everything looks very similar to the original match day, for what I can remember of that day after all this time.

And what a match it was! We made it! We are not being relegated! I don't remember running so much in the hundreds of matches played in my whole life, or making so much tackles in one match. Mathew, another fat old guy playing his last match, got the ball a couple of metres from the goal line, turned slightly his head to the right and I was there, he passed me the ball, I made one step forward and returned the ball to him, and the fat bastard just had to dive and score the first and last try of his embarrassing playing career.

Made in the USA
Columbia, SC
05 April 2025

56105168R00037